Attention
all Super Hero S...
Look for these items when you r...
Can you guess which of your favorite
characters use them?

HAMMER

SURFBOARD

SHIELD

BOW AND ARROW

Little, Brown and Company

Hachette Book Group
237 Park Avenue, New York, NY 10017
Visit our website at www.lb-kids.com

LB kids is an imprint of Little, Brown and Company. The LB kids name and logo are trademarks of Hachette Book Group, Inc.

First edition: April 2010
10 9 8 7 6 5 4

ISBN: 978-0-316-05572-7

www.marvelkids.com

Printed in the U.S.A.

MEET THE SUPER HERO SQUAD!

by Lucy Rosen
illustrated by Dario Bruela
and Miguel Spadafino

LITTLE, BROWN & COMPANY
LB kids

Super Hero City is the home of
the world's most amazing adventurers.
They are strong.
They are brave.
They are the Super Hero Squad!

Whenever the city is in danger,
it's up to the Super Hero Squad
to protect it.

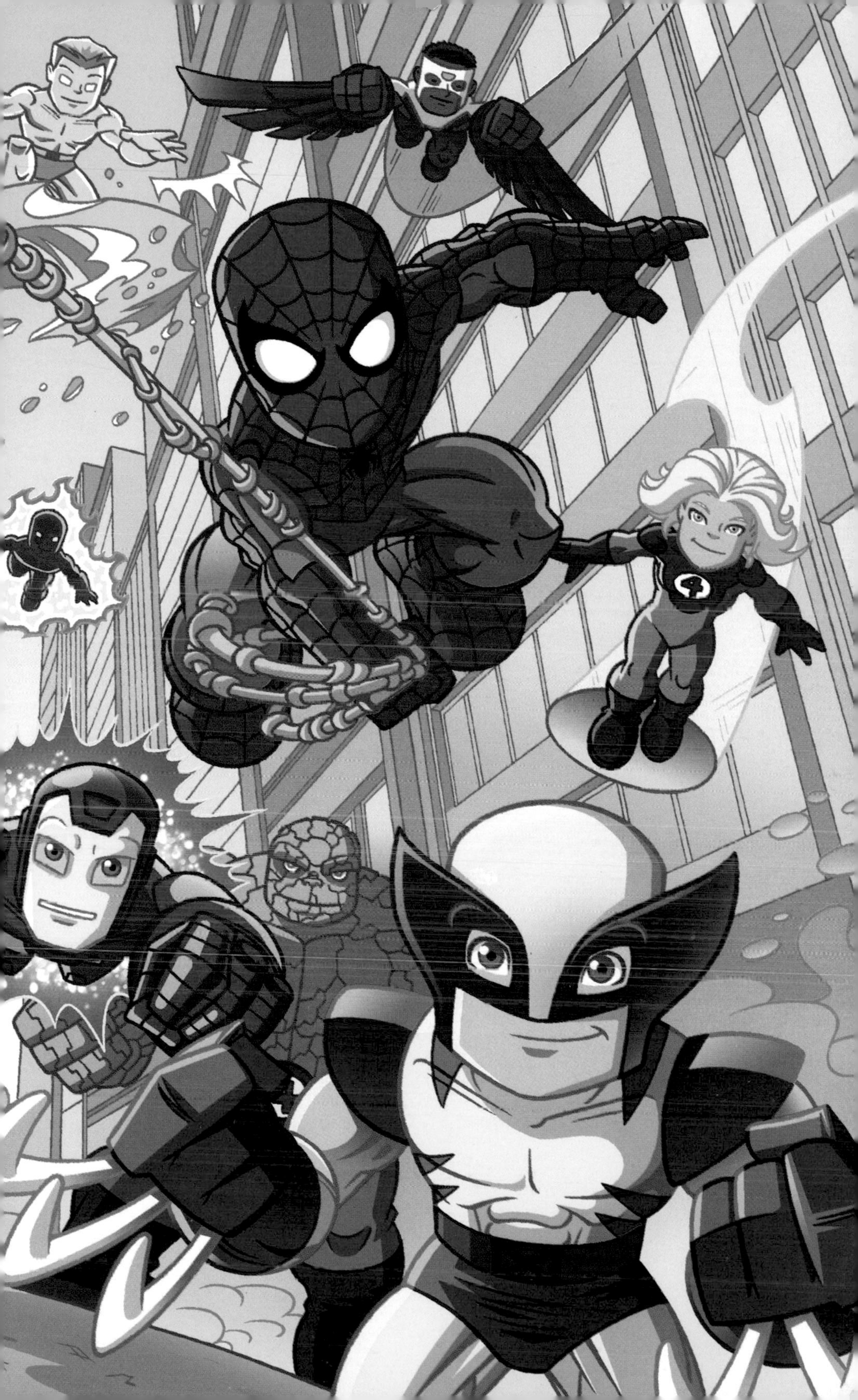

Iron Man is the leader of the Squad.
If bad guys come looking for a fight,
they need to watch out!
Iron Man wears a suit of armor
that no enemy can destroy.

Iron Man has an invention
for every emergency.
"Armor up!" he says.

Wolverine is always ready
to leap into action.
He is the toughest hero
in town.

With his metal claws,
Wolverine climbs a tree
to rescue a cat.
It's a good thing he can heal
from any scratch!

Hulk is stronger than anyone.
He is a great hero,
and a good friend, too.
Just don't get him angry!
Hulk smashes things
when his temper explodes.

Silver Surfer rides the skies
on his superpowered surfboard.
"Space out and surf up!" he says as he
zigs and zags through outer space.

Everyone in Super Hero City
knows who Thor is.
With his hammer in hand,
he is hard to miss.

Thor has lots of tricks
when it comes to battling bad guys.
Not only is he strong and powerful,
but he can control the weather, too!

CRASH!
That sound means
Thing is on his way.
A shower of rocks falls off
this mighty hero's back
whenever he moves a muscle.

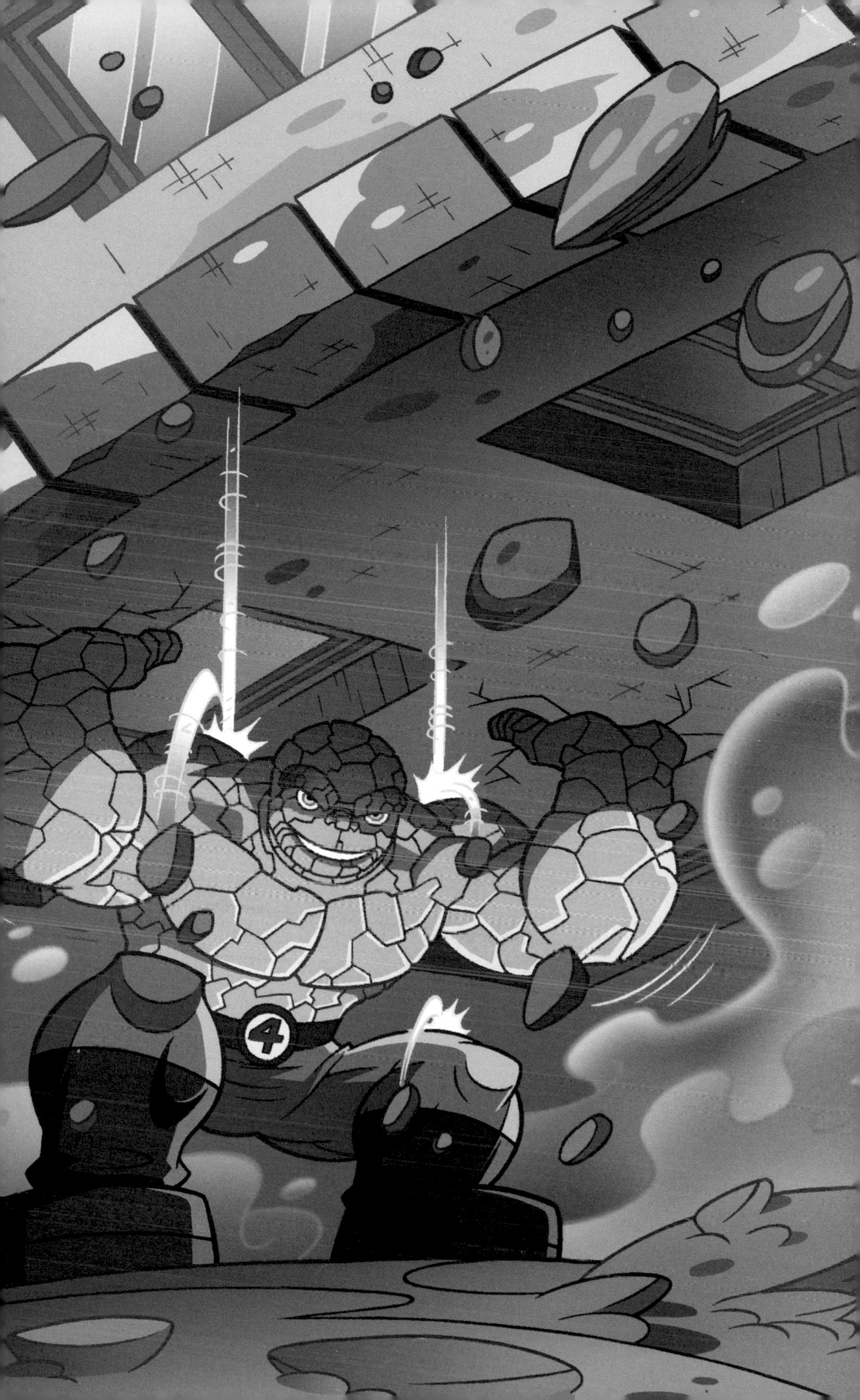

Hawkeye is always right on target
with his bow and arrow.
He never backs away from a challenge
and is always up for action.

If Invisible Woman is out of sight,
everyone should be careful.
She's either making bad guys disappear,
or she's pulling a prank on the Squad!

Human Torch is Invisible
Woman's little brother.
He can shoot flames
and zoom through the sky.
Things always heat up
when Human Torch is around.

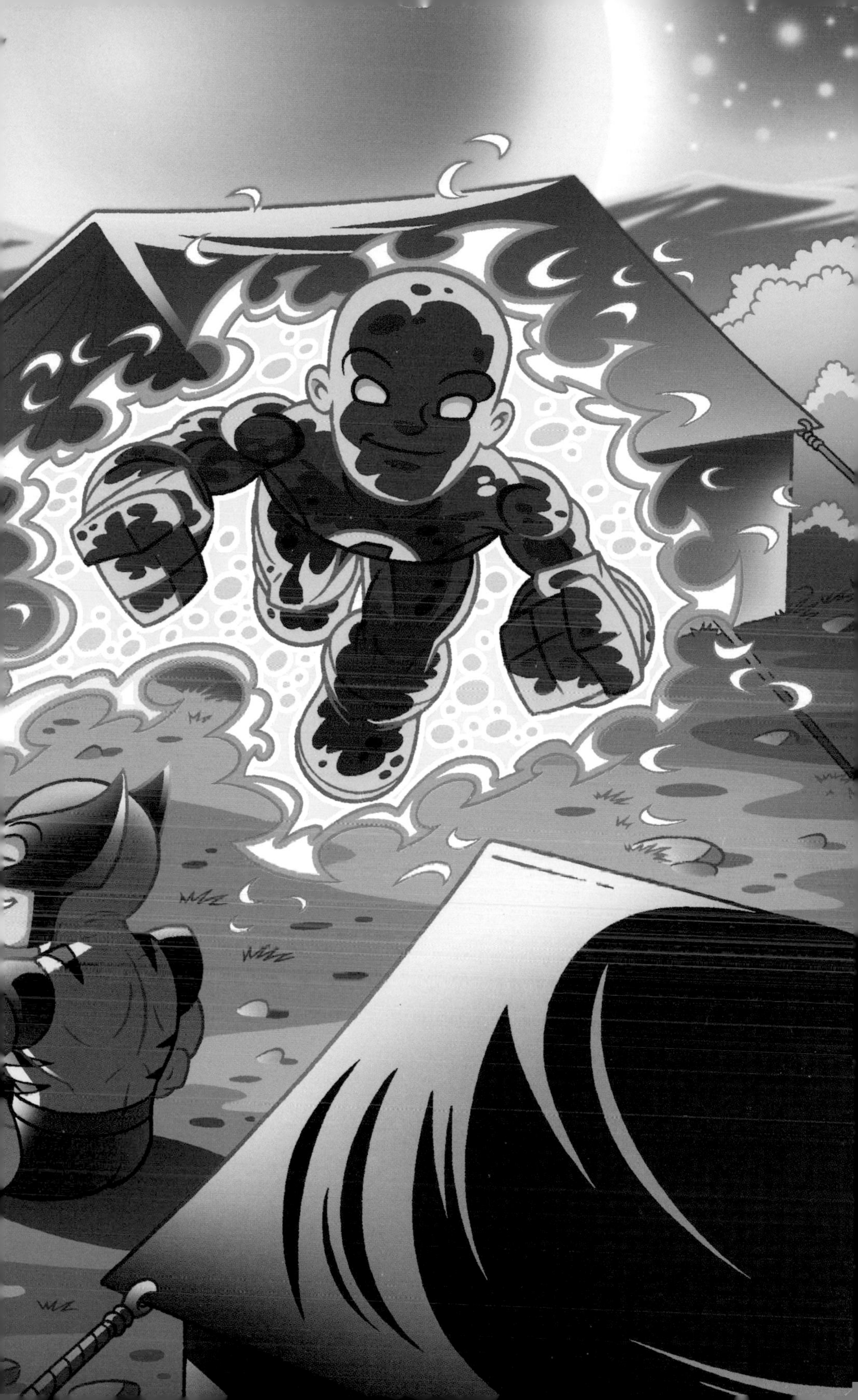

Iceman might be young,
but villains are no match for his
blasts of chilly wind and ice!
Iceman is the coolest member
of the Squad.

Captain America is true blue
and loyal to his fellow heroes.
His shield is superstrong
and protects him from any foe.

Nothing stands between
Cyclops and his friends.
He keeps the Squad out of trouble
and always plays by the rules.

Falcon is the Squad's best soldier. He soars through the sky with his "Hard Light" wings, and he can even talk to birds. Just don't tell anyone that Falcon is afraid of heights!

Mr. Fantastic is supersmart, superfast, and superstretchy. His elastic body can twist into any shape.

Mr. Fantastic loves a good mystery.
If there is a problem to solve,
Mr. Fantastic is ready to
stretch his imagination and solve it!

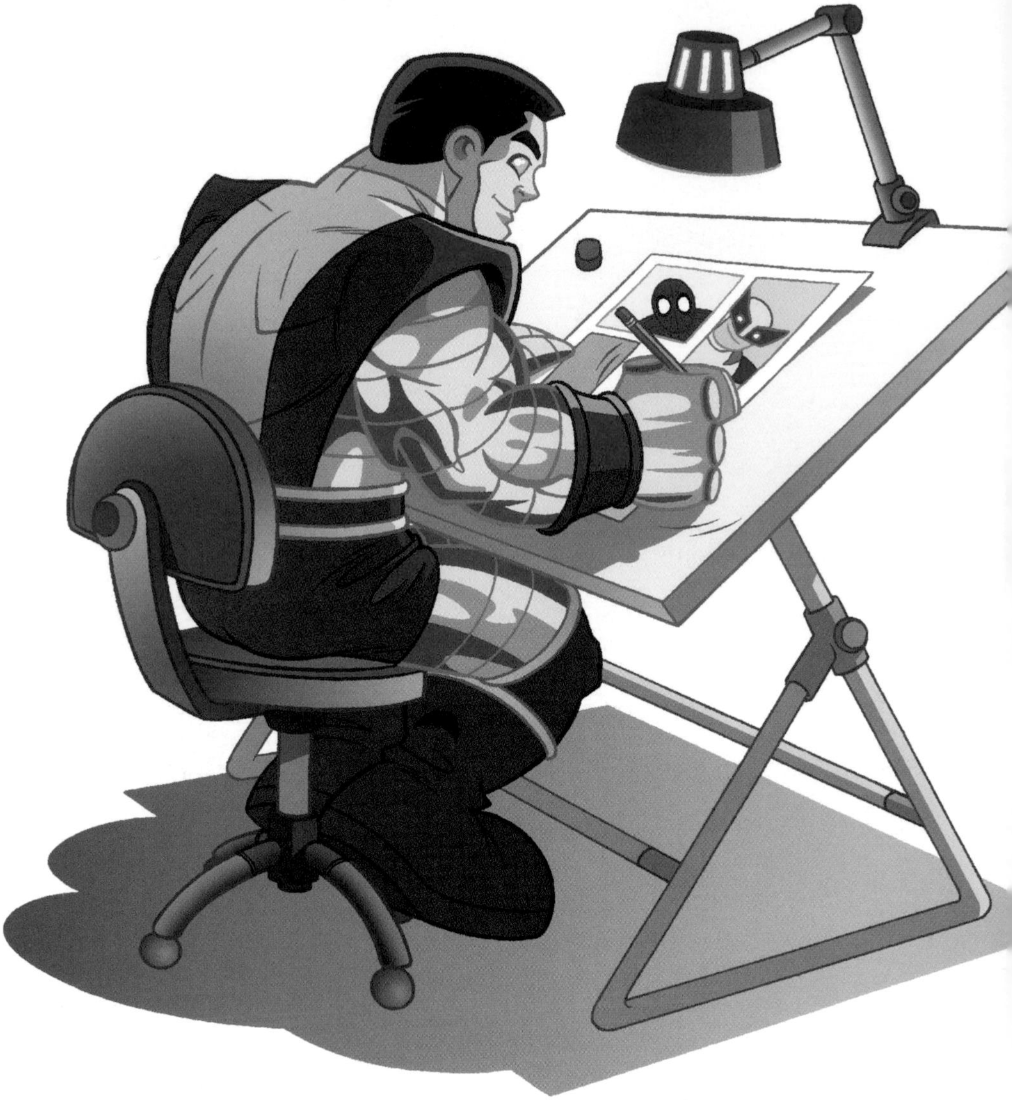

When Colossus isn't strong as steel
to fight a bad guy,
he is drawing a comic strip.
Colossus is the most artistic
Super Hero the Squad has ever seen.

Dr. Strange knows everything
about spells and magic.
He can kick out evil forces
from Super Hero City, for good!

If he isn't busy protecting
New York from danger,
Spider-Man swings
by Super Hero City
to lend a helping hand.

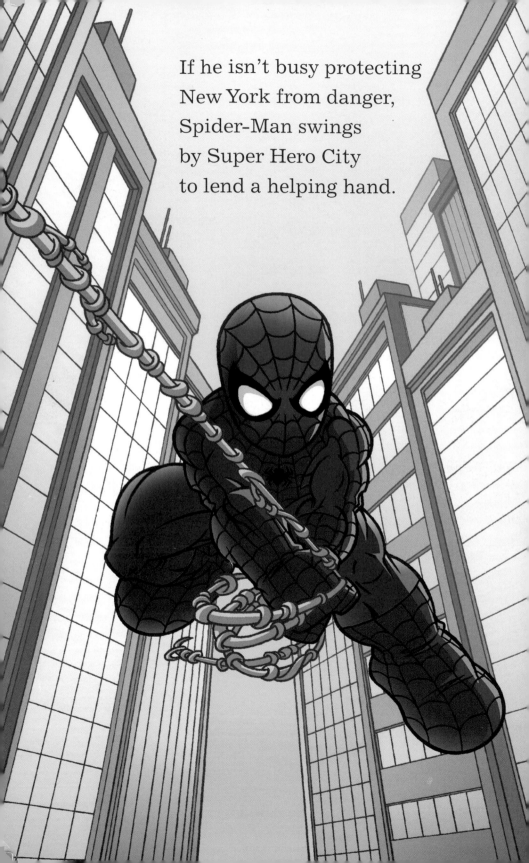

Reptil is part boy, part dinosaur.
With the help of his ancient sunstone,
Reptil can grow pterodactyl wings
or stegosaurus spikes in no time!

"Listen up, Super Heroes!"
yells General "Thunderbolt" Ross.
When this grumpy guy gives an order,
the Squad knows something is up.

"Dr. Doom and his evildoers
are planning an attack,"
growls the General.
"We've got to protect our city!"

30

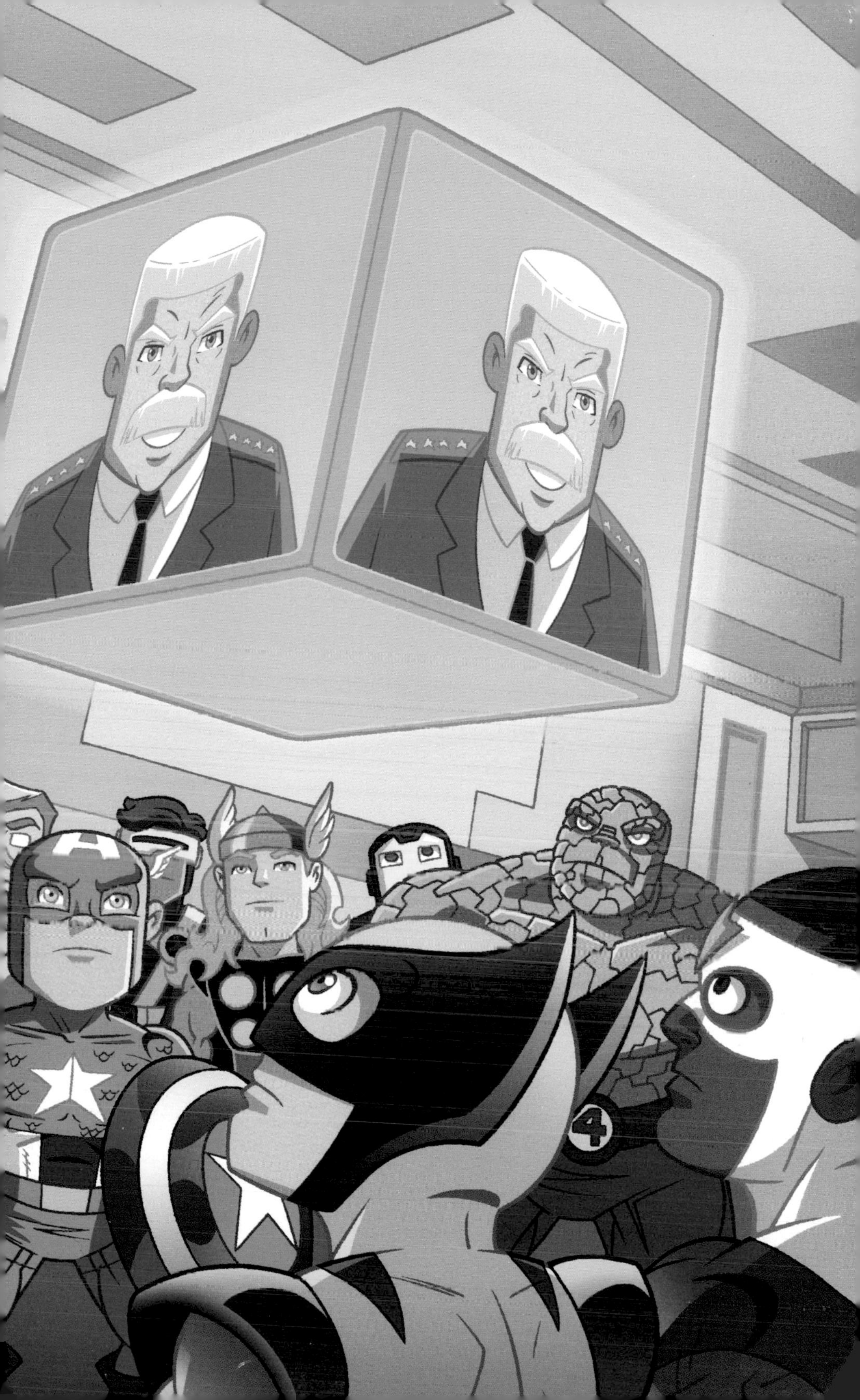

The Super Hero Squad
knows just what that means.
"Time to Hero Up!"
they shout.